THE *Opportunity*

A NOVELLA

IAN
BESTSELLING AUTHOR
SCHRAUTH

CHAPTER 1

"Mommy Tsunami, out!" my phone stated before the screen went dim.

I was watching another one of Savannah Marie's videos while waiting for a call to come in.

This was the last video in her series, and it left me...bored. The call volume was low, and I haven't received a call in about 30 minutes.

Working virtually sucks, but it gave me time to watch my favorite YouTubers while on the clock.

When the next set of videos popped on my screen, I got a call.

I unmuted my mic and clicked the green "ACCEPT" button.

"Thank you for calling Veri..."

"This is the fifth call I've made to you guys! I don't want to hear it!" They yelled. "I need a supervisor, NOW!"

Oh God...

"Well, before I can transfer you, I need to know who I'm talking to. May I have your first and last name and--"

"Karen Jones! Now transfer me to your supervisor!"

"I also need your phone number, ma'am." I stated.

After a few minutes of going back and forth, I could tell not only that she was about to go off on me, but I could hear a click in the phone system, like someone was listening in.

"This is obviously above your pay grade, so I need a supervisor NOW before heads start rolling!"

Well, time to get a supervisor…

Not because she requested it, but because she's threatening us…

"Okay ma'am. Since you're sending us death threats, I will get my supervisor on the call with me so we can contact your local authorities. Please be on hold." I stated and immediately placed her on hold.

I then got a direct message from my supervisor. It seems like she was listening to the call.

"Name and phone that popped up?" The message asked.

I gave her the customer's name, and the phone number that came up in the phone system, and after a few seconds, my supervisor stated, "Transfer her to me. 9th call in a row and 3rd threat in a row."

I pulled up my supervisor and transferred the caller to her. God, this has been a bad day…

Not only were call volumes out of the roof, but customers have been *assholes!*

It's like…Why would you be an ass to the person that is trying to help you!

It was my time to clock off, so I logged out of the phone system and clocked off. I just sat there, staring at my screen, feeling like I was brain dead.

God, I need a new job…

* * *

I was sitting with my mother, eating dinner later that night. I was talking to her about my day and the last customer.

"God, people suck!" She said and rolled her eyes. She took a bite of her asparagus and said, "You need to find a new job, Ali. Especially in the field of marketing"

"I know," I stated. "I've been putting out my resume, but nobody wants to give me a chance."

"Trust me, someone will give you a chance." She stated and took a drink.

CHAPTER 2

I woke up the next morning and just stared at the ceiling. I had to go to school today….

I better get my social media kick in, first...

I picked up my phone and opened up Tik Tok.

As I was scrolling through videos, there was one that struck my attention. Her location was in Saint Louis -- same as mine -- and she was saying something about money management.

Knowing me and my spending habits, I needed to watch that…

She was talking about how she thought the viewer (me) was watching because we needed money management, and how she had an opportunity to work from her phone, work her own hours, and make as much as she wanted to, and said she was hiring!

She also stated about how she only had two spots left on her team!

That sounded good to me!

She said something about an application in her bio, so I went to her bio, and looked at the *GOOGLE FORM…*

My brain was tired, so I wasn't paying attention to the major red flags in this situation, like asking for my Instagram handle, and wanting to know if 50k monthly would help me…

I was thinking "If she can do this, I can too!"

I finished filling out the application, and my alarm went off.

Well, time to get up and get ready…

I got up from my bed, put my hair in a messy bun, and got on some clean clothes. I grabbed my phone and my backpack, and headed downstairs to make myself some breakfast.

When I got down to the kitchen, I noticed on my phone I received an Instagram message from someone.

****Hey! Thank you for filling out my application! I'm McKayla Payton! Do you have some time to chat over the phone? ****

The red flags were starting to kick in, and I was starting to regret what I did…

I texted her my number, and she IMMEDIATELY gave me a call…

"This is Ali," I stated.

"Hey! It's McKayla! Is now a good time to talk?" She asked.

"Yeah, I'm just making breakfast!" I stated.

"Good! So, like I said, thank you for filling out my application for this opportunity! With this company, you will be selling top-quality products and making an unlimited amount of commission off it! We work from our phones, and we make as much money as we want! The possibilities are endless!" She stated. "You can also hire your own people and build your team!"

Wait…

Is this a pyramid scheme?

"This sounds like a pyramid scheme," I stated. "What's the company name?"

"Well, pyramid schemes are illegal, so I can assure you it's definitely not that!" She stated and giggled. "If you need some time to think about it, it's totally fine!"

She didn't answer the question!

"What's the company name?" I asked, again.

"It's called ItWorks!, and if you need some time to think about all this, that's fine! Just giving you a heads up to not listen to the people online because a lot of people hate on the business."

"Yeah, I'll need some time to think about this," I stated. "Can I get back with you after class?"

"Yeah! What time do you get out of class? I think I saw you go to the same school as you! Do you want to meet up and talk a little more about it?"

Wait…

I didn't state on the app where I went to school!

How did she know?!

"How did you know we went to the same school?" I asked.

There was a pause, before she said, "Because you just told me! But yeah, we'll catch up later! Bye!" and hung up.

At that time, all of my red flags were blaring.

Yeah, I'm gonna look up this ItWorks! company, and see what people had to say...

CHAPTER 3

On my way to school, I was listening to some podcasts about ItWorks, and what some people had to say about the company.

I tell you what; those podcasts had good things to say about the company.

I have NO idea if they were a part of ItWorks, but all the podcasts I found were good…

I arrived on campus and got out of the car. The weather was very cool, as we just got off Spring Break.

I locked my car and headed to building A, where my business development class was.

I was about ten minutes early, and the professor uses that time to go over anything business-related that we might have. Mainly to keep us focused for that day in class.

He usually lets us have a debate with each other and he corrects us when we're wrong, but mostly has us answer a question on the board.

I had a few questions for my professor….

When I sat my stuff down in my seat, I brought out my laptop and looked around. I was the only one in there, with the exception of the professor.

"Professor Casva, I have a few questions, and possibly a suggestion for this morning's topic," I stated.

"I'll take the discussion topic now, but keep the questions to yourself until everyone shows up. That way others can know the answer if they have the same question, and to start us off"

"Sure. The topic has to do with companies like ItWorks!"

He looked a little surprised -- in a good way -- and went up the board. He wrote in big letters "TODAY'S DISCUSSION: MULTI-LEVEL MARKETING"

Is THAT what it's officially called?

Huh...interesting…

* * *

When enough students piled in, he closed the door, and stated, "As you read on the board, the discussion is Multi-Level marketing. I think Ali has a few questions to start us off. Go ahead, Ali."

I hate being put in the spotlight…

"Well, I was listening to some recommended podcasts in the car, and they were talking about how good the business is. Is it really that good?"

He nodded, and the girl in the back of the class -- I think her name is Darlene -- spoke.

"Yes, the business is AMAZING! I get to do this during the nooks and crannies of my day, and when I want to make some extra money on the--"

She was interrupted by another girl named Isabella. "That is IF you're the top 1% of the company. According to the FTC, 99.6% of people in these schemes lose money or fail. The business is shaped as an illegal--"

"Excuse me," Darlene stated. "Let me just state that multi-level marketing is an investment! The products that we sell will—"

"Placeholder products," the quiet kid mentioned. "Those are only there to cover up the fact that they're slimy and disgusting."

Darlene looked at him in disgust and stated, "Facts don't care about your feelings!"

"If you're so into the facts let's look at the FTC Appendix 7e," Isabella stated and brought out her computer.

"While you look for that *fake* news, it's worth pointing out that pyramid schemes are illegal, so there is *no* way to classify us multi-level-marketers as a pyramid scheme."

"So is speeding, but that happens on the daily." The quiet kid stated. "How do you explain that?"

She just huffed. "You can't win with *bullies*."

"Not bullying you. Just stating the truth," He clapped back.

"Here it is!" Isabella stated. "According to the FTC Appendix 7e, 99.6% of MLM participants lose money, and you have a better chance at making money gambling in Las Vegas than you do in a scummy MLM. Plus, you have a better chance at a *legitimate* small business, than an MLM!"

"But we ARE small business owners!" Darlene stated.

Isabella raised an eyebrow. "No, you're not. You paid to become a commission-only salesperson. If I buy products from Walmart, I don't consider myself a 'Walmart Business owner'. That's not ethical; just like Scentsy."

"Which we all can tell you sell because of how you smell," The quiet kid butted in.

Damn…

This is getting heated.

"Like I keep saying, *facts* don't care about your *feelings*!" She stated to the quiet kid again. "And also, why is *Network Marketing* the second-highest industry in the nation? I mean, you have the potential to make UNLIMITED sales! You can't do that in your scummy nine-to-five" She asked. "That makes it the PERFECT investment!"

"First off, it's *multi-level marketing.* Calling a turd a bar of gold doesn't change the fact it's a turd."

"Let me stop you guys. I can say that Multi-Level Marketing is NOT the largest money-maker in the world. That has the place of a Cardiologist." Professor Casva stated.

"Yes. And it's not even considered a career unless you're a part of the top 0.01% of people that *actually* make money," Isabella stated. "And plus, if it's the *perfect investment,* why does the FTC appendix 7e even *exist?*"

"That study is flawed! They are considering distributors who try to sell and distributors only in it for the discount!" She stated.

"And you know why people say that?" Isabella asked.

"They say that bec-"

"Because they don't want to deal with people telling them they failed at their quote-on-quote business." The quiet kid stated again. "Sounds like facts don't care about YOUR feelings."

"And we're also forgetting that 80 percent of women who are millionaires do so through Network marketing!" She stated. I could tell she was on her last straw.

"Oh, that statistic is *supposed* to say '80 percent of people who are successful in network marketing are women. You're saying an *actual* statistic wrong." Isabella stated. "Stop lying!"

Darlene packed up her things, pulled out a business card, and sat it on my desk. "I'm sorry you all had a bad experience in your MLMs, but I can tell you that Sentsy is NOT like that! Good day to you guys!"

As she was heading to the door, the quiet kid yelled, "99.6% of people had a bad experience?"

She gave him the middle finger and walked out.

CHAPTER 4

Professor Casva let us out a little early today. We don't know why, but I guess he had to write up an incident report for what happened before class started.

Who knows…

I was one of the first to walk out of the class, and as I was walking down the hall, I got a DM from McKayla.

Before I could even read her message, I could feel myself run into someone….

I didn't see who it was at first, but I was hoping it wasn't Darlene…

When I looked up, I saw the body of who I ran into.

Holy…shit….

He looked like the literal textbook definition of sexy, from his thick, short, brown hair, to his 6 pack, to the bulge in his pants!

Holy fucking shit…

I'm not the one to believe in love at first sight, but DAMN!

"I'm SO sorry about this!" I said and got on my knees to pick up my stuff.

"It's okay!" he said, and picked up the last of his things.

Instead of just heading off, he helped me pick up the rest of my things. Luckily, there wasn't a single soul heading the direction I was going, so we picked up my stuff pretty quickly.

"Thank you," I stated. "You didn't have to do that."

"It's okay. I love helping people! It's what I do for a living!" He stated and smiled.

A living?

Maybe I could ask him to hire me!

"What do you do?" I asked.

"Well, I work for a health and wellness company, selling stuff. I get to set my own hours and work when I want. If you want to, I can add you on Facebook, and we can discuss it further. I have to get to class soon."

That would be good. He could send me a link to apply, and I would be able to work around my schooling!"

"Sure!" I stated.

He handed me a business card with his name on it and smiled. "We have a business meeting coming up tonight over zoom. Would you be interested in coming?"

Business meeting?

What the hell?

I was too starstruck to even care at this point.

"Sure," I replied.

"Okay! I'll let you know more over Facebook! Bye!" He said and walked off.

As I was walking to my car, I got a friend request from someone.

"Hayden Morris had requested to add you"

I tell you what, Hayden. You're hot stuff!

CHAPTER 5

I decided to give the meeting a shot and go. I mean, the worst that could happen is I'm out for a couple of hours.

At least I hope that's all I'm out…

I was putting on some of my good Bath and Body Works body spray when mom walked by the bathroom. She looked at how fancy I was dressed and asked, "Where are you going, dressed like that?"

"I'm going to some business meeting that someone I met at school is hosting," I replied and turned around. "How do I look?"

"Well, you look very…businessesy." she stated as I walked past her. "I have to warn you about something though.

I paused right before I put my first show on. "What is it?"

"Well, do you remember our old church? Saved by Grace Lutheran?"

How could I NOT forget about them?

"Yeah, what about it?" I asked.

"Well, they got involved in some sort of company that would help them pay off their debt. It was a get-rich-quick scheme, and I forgot what the company name was. All I know is that they were constantly recruiting us when you were younger, saying they were hiring for a 'brand ambassador' role."

Wait…

I don't remember *that* happening!

I was too curious about the event to even care about something that my old, toxic church had to do.

* * *

I arrived at the house that I was directed to go to, and strangely enough, it was in my neighborhood…

I STILL didn't know who the hell they were…

I waited in my car, and I then heard a knock on my window!

I jumped out of fear and looked out.

McKayla?

I rolled down my window, and said, "Hey, aren't you McKayla?"

"Yeah! Who invited you? I was gonna invite you, but I found another friend to come along!" she stated. She didn't sound angry about the situation, as I imagined she would.

"A guy I met at school named...Hayden??" I said, second-guessing myself. "Yeah, Hayden."

She grew a smile on her face. "Awesome! So, this is Hayden's house! Wanna come in with us?"

As I got out of the car with pepper spray in my pocket, someone else walked up.

"Hey Ali!" The other person stated. "Amazing to see you here!"

Holy fucking shit...

It was Darlene!

What the *fuck* is she doing here?!

Maybe she came along to get out of her Multi-Level Marketing company.

"Hey!" I greeted as we were walking up to the house. "What brings you along?"

"Well, I want to prove to everyone in that hateful class that MLMs are NOT what those ass holes think!"

Honestly, a red flag would have popped up in my brain, but I was too focused on Hayden's hot body as we walked up to him in front of the doorway."

"Hateful class?" McKayla asked. "And you didn't tell me you're in Scentsy!

"Yeah, these haters in our Introduction to Business Logic class were bullying me and my business, and saying how Scentsy is a scam, FTC shit, yadda yadda yadda." she said. "Isn't that right Ali?"

The fuck are you asking *me* for?

"Sure?" I said, questioning myself.

"Don't listen to those haters. They just need to be cut out of your life. I would drop that class since we all know the fact that college is the *true* pyramid scheme!" McKayla stated as we walked up the porch.

Wait...

How is *college* a pyramid scheme?

Nevermind....

"Hey ladies! Glad you could make it to this business meeting!" Hayden stated.

"Hey Hayden!" McKayla greeted as we all walked in. "We were just talking about the bullies in Ali's and Darlene's business class!" She said.

We walked into their beautiful kitchen, and there were a BUNCH of products on their table and counter! From what looked like hot tea, to what looked like little yogurt smoothie bottles with a paper sign that said "Toxic sludge killer!" and large bags of what looked like protein powder...

"Take a look around before the meeting!" A lady stated. She looked like Hayden's mother.

I walked up to the bag of what looked like protein powder and read the label.

"ItWorks! Keto Coffee. Put more in your cup!"

What the ACTUAL fuck is Keto Coffee?

What's the difference between *actual* coffee and *this?*

Who knows, but I bet it tastes...interesting...

"That's our famous best-selling Coffee!" McKayla stated behind me. "It's SO yummy! Wanna try some?"

Now?

It's, like, seven-thirty in the evening!

"No thanks, I don't drink coffee after 5 PM," I stated, which was a lie.

SOME nights, I drink coffee to stay up and do my homework, and I have a pot ready for me when I get home because my manager puts me on the night shift on a SCHOOL night...

"Okay!" she stated and looked behind her to another room. "The meeting's starting soon! We better get in there! Don't want to miss *anything* they say!"

Who are *they*, Jesus?

CHAPTER 6

We walked into the family room, and I saw there were a lot of people in there. A lot of them were females, and only a few (around three, including Hayden and an older man) were males.

I sat down on the couch in the middle of McKayla and Hayden, and I saw someone turn on an Apple TV and was mirroring their Mac.

I could only see a glimpse of their background, but it looked like a family photo with Hayden on the left side.

I looked at the lady on the laptop, and it hit me.

She was his mother, and the older man was his father!

Was he an only child?

"Someone got up from their seat and grabbed a remote from Hayden's mother, and went up to the front.

"Welcome! If you don't know who I am, my name is Merik Morris, and I am a Diamond with this business! We will be talking about a lot of things about this business, so I hope you all brought your business notebooks with you."

Business notebooks?

I haven't learned *that* in business class…

McKayla pulled out something from her large purse and handed it to me.

A dollar store notebook and a dollar store pen…

The only reason why I knew they were from the dollar store was because I use them for school….

"Thank you!" I whispered.

"No problem! Once you sign up with us, you'll need this to take notes at future meetings," she stated.

In the notebook she gave me, there were notes she had already written in there for me.

I decided to look through the notes later, and then I went to the next blank page and started writing down what they were saying.

"Now, we are going to be discussing recruiting for your business today! I can promise you that once you recruit three people and teach them to do the same, you will be sitting on piles and piles of money!" he stated and clicked on the remote.

On the next slide, it showed what looked like the corporate hierarchy, with someone at the top, three people at the bottom, and three people under those three people."

It looked like a...triangle...

"Now, since all of you are right here," he stated and pointed to the top of the triangle. "Once you hire three people to sell under you, and they recr...hire three people under them, money just goes up the latter, and into your pockets."

Wait just *one second*...

If someone signs me up here, would I be at the very top or in the middle of this very familiar shape?

I'm *honestly confused.*

I raised my hand and Merik looked at me. "Write down your questions, and I'll answer them at the end."

Okay?

Strange…

He clicked the button on his remote and went to the next slide. "Now, I know a lot of you are wondering some things that can help you hire brand ambassadors under you, and we have compiled some of the best tactics throughout the entire company. You all should be VERY honored because this comes from all of the diamonds in this company!"

Oh *wow*…

And I don't mean that in a surprising way…

I mean that in a "I'm being sarcastic because I'm bored as fuck" way.

As he was showing us the tactics, all I could think about was "why the fuck would someone say that to another human?"

I don't know if that is the Libertarian coming out of me, but still!

One of them was to ask new mothers something about staying home with their kids while working!

WHAT?!

Before I could write down some examples I was thinking of, he was already presenting the next slide!

I was hurting up to write down some examples when a piece of folded paper landed on my notebook.

What question did you have earlier?

It was from McKayla's side, so I wrote down the question I had earlier, and gave it back to her.

She looked at the question, looked at me, pointed at Merik, and continued to write down notes in her notebook.

Thank you for dodging my questions, McKayla…

As I was writing down the notes, I heard someone get up from the couch.

It was Hayden…

Apparently, he was going to be speaking!

I watched him walk up to the front (when I mean watched him, I mean just stare at his sexy, round ass), and grab the remote from the man. The man sat down in Hayden's seat, and Hayden stared to tell his success story.

I should have guessed that because the PowerPoint screen read "Success Story: Hayden Morris."

I closed my notebook and just listened to him. I wasn't *really* paying attention to his words, but I was paying attention to the large bulge in his professional, black pants.

Holy shit, I think he's around seven inches!

As Hayden was telling his story and I was making up *very* dirty things, McKayla nudged me.

"Hey, why aren't you taking notes!" she whispered.

"Sorry," I stated and opened up my notebook.

CHAPTER 7

"So yeah, get with the person that brought you, and let's see what we can do to get you into this business!" Merik stated as he walked up. Hayden just got done talking, and everyone was getting up to stretch.

Holy shit....

I think he talked for about an hour about himself.

I didn't think I could daydream of him fucking me for that long!

McKayla got up and walked over to Hayden, and they started talking. I was just looking at them as they were discussing something.

I got up, stretched, and walked up to them. Hayden looked at me and smiled.

That smile…

That damn smile!

It shot me in the chest and left me starstruck!

"McKayla and I were just talking, and if you want to sign up under McKayla, that would be fine."

I'm not too sure about this whole "signing up under someone"…

"Well, I'd have to think about it." I stated.

"Tell you what. I'll give you my number, and we can talk about it. How does that sound? You already have McKalyla's number, since you filled out her job application."

Yeah….*job application…*

More like "filled out her Google Form"….

Because that's what it was!

Hayden gave me a business card, entered his number into my phone, and texted him a "hello!"

"I'm gonna go ahead and get going. Do you wanna come with me, Ali?" McKayla asked.

"I think I'll stay and look at the products a little bit more," I stated. I was *waiting* for him to take me to his room and rearrange my guts.

Damn, I'm horny tonight…

"That's cool. There *are* a few things I need to show you anyway." Hayden stated. "Follow me."

I said goodbye to McKayla and followed him into the kitchen. He pulled out something and handed it to me. "Just because I think you're a nice girl, I wanted to give you this."

It was an ItWorks Blender bottle…

It looked cheap, and I bet they marked the price up on it.…

I grabbed the blender bottle, from his soft hands, and looked at it.

It has the ItWorks Logo splattered on the front…

"Thanks!" I stared and smiled, hoping my smile was just as good as his.

"No problem," he stated and smiled back. "Look, it's getting late so you better get going. Do you want to take a keto coffee packet with you?"

Why is he giving me all this free stuff?

Is he trying to portray a message?

"Sure!" I stated.

He ran to the cabinet and came back with about three packets of the keto coffee. "Try it and tell us what you think!"

"Thank you!" I stated as he walked me out.

"No, thank *you* for coming!"

* * *

When I walked into my condo, I knocked on mom's door, and said, "Hey, I'm home."

"Later than I thought. How was it?" she asked.

"It was good."

"Did they pitch you anything?"

"No, it was mainly going over a trip they went on," I lied. "I got some free samples, too!"

I could hear her get up from her bed, and saw her open the door. "What type of samples?"

"Some keto coffee," she stated.

She raised an eyebrow. "*Keto* coffee?"

I nodded.

"How can it be *keto?* All coffee is, is water and coffee bean juice."

"Don't know, but I'm about to try it." I stated and walked to the kitchen.

Mom followed me, and said, "this I gotta see."

I poured a cup of regular coffee into my least favorite mug and poured the packet of keto coffee in with it.

"What does it smell like?" She asked.

I smelt it, and oh...my...god...

It smelt like a fucking farm...

"It smells like..." I started to say and smelt it again. "A farm...."

"A *farm?!*" Mom asked, grabbed the cup, and smelt it. "Smells like fucking farm soil."

I put the cup in the microwave and heated up the cup.

When it was done, I pulled out the cup and took a sip.

Ewe...

It tastes worse than it smells...

Apparently, I made a face that made mom laugh, and she said, "it can't be *that* bad!" and grabbed the cup from me.

She took a sip and poured the cup down the drain. "Yeah, that shit sucks..."

"Well, I have three more packets where that came from," I stated and put the packets on the counter.

"I have a *perfect* home for them!" she said and grabbed the packets. She went over to the trash can and threw them out. "There we go, they're home now!"

Nice!

I poured myself an ACTUAL cup of coffee, said goodnight to mom, and went to my room to work....

CHAPTER 8

It was around 1:30 in the morning, and I was two-thirds finished with my shift!

Thank the lord!

While I was wrapping up my last call, I was also swiping on Tinder. I know I wasn't supposed to be on my phone during a call, but I couldn't help it....

Before I hit the button to go to the next call, I swiped one more unattractive guy until it popped up with a "Secret admirer" popup and it directed me to choose a blurred profile.

I LOVE doing these!

I clicked on the one with what looked like a shirtless guy, and it was a match, to my surprise!

The only problem: It was Hayden.

Holy...shit...

I JUST spoke with him about joining his business, and here he is liking my profile!

I looked at the match details, and noticed he Super Liked me!

If he's into me as much as I'm into him, we should get along *well!*

As I was taking my next call, I received a message from him.

Hey, I know you!

The call just ended, and I picked up my phone and messaged him.

Yeah lol whats up?

He was typing up a reply when I received a call.

As I was helping the customer, I was in the middle of explaining how to reset network settings on your iPhone, when I noticed a message on mine.

*** Nothing much. I swiped right before I met you, and you swiped right just now. I didn't know you liked me lol ***

Well shit…

I've been caught…but I think I have "looking for friends" in my bio.

**** *I'm only looking for friends here. I swipe right on everyone.* ****

Yeah, I use Tinder for friends, and I have my profile set to Bisexual, so I can see both males and females.

He didn't respond after that, so I continued working my shift.

* * *

I finished my shift at around 5-o'clock in the morning. God, I was tired.

I was so tired; I had to look at my phone to see what day it was.

Yup, Tuesday…and still no reply from Hayden.

I got in the shower and washed up. I just let the water hit my face, as I was about to fall asleep.

Good thing I like my showers so hot, it burns my skin.

I got out of the shower and got dressed in some casual clothes.

Today I had my hybrid math class, so I had to go to school to be on the computer and learn math….then go home and go on the computer to work at 2….

Ugh, I *have* to get another job…

Preferably one that I can do on *my own time!*

I grabbed a granola bar from the cabinet, said bye to mom, and headed out to my car.

As I was driving to school, I was thinking of the different types of jobs I could do.

I was weighing my options between ItWorks, and possibly a different call center.

Why would I want to be under the boss of someone else, when I could be my own boss, make my own hours, and make uncapped income?

I mean, that's what they promised at the meeting I went to!

When I arrived at college, I pulled out my phone and texted McKayla.

"Hey, get me signed up."

CHAPTER 9

McKayla didn't text me at *all* during my math class, and I ended up almost falling asleep through it.

When the class was over, I packed up my things and walked out.

As I was walking to the cafeteria to get some *actual* food, I bumped into Hayden.

"Hey Ali! Did you try the keto coffee I gave you?"

I didn't want to tell him that it tasted like *shit,* because he might not accept me for it.

"I didn't," I stated. "I plan on doing it after school."

"That's fine," He stated and started to walk beside me. "It tastes *really* good, so I would try it as soon as possible!"

I beg to differ, but okay…

"I gotcha," I stated. "I contacted McKayla to get me signed up."

He grew a smile on his face. "You did? Awesome! I'm stoked that you're taking a leap into starting your own business!"

I had a bad gut feeling about this whole process, but it's probably because I'm hungry.

"Yeah," I stated. "Well, I'm getting hungry so I better get something to eat."

"Okay! I'll see you on the flip side, teammate!" he said and walked away. While he was walking, he pumped his fist.

Red flag number one…

* * *

While I was eating a slice of pizza in the school cafeteria, I got a call from McKayla.

"Hello?"

"Hey, are you out of class now? I'm in the school cafeteria if you want to get signed up."

Girl…

It took you FOREVER to respond…

I looked around, and I saw her two tables down from me.

"Look behind you," I stated.

She swiftly turned her head, hung up, grabbed her stuff, and walked over to my table.

Like, did I invite you over?

"Hey, what's up?" She asked and sat down.

"Nothing much, just eating lunch," I stated.

"Once you sign up, you *need* to get some of our Fat Fighters, so those fats don't make you...you know." she stated and opened up her laptop.

Was she calling me *fat*?

"Calling me fat?" I asked,

"No" she stated, not even looking up from her laptop. "I'm just filling in my information so they know who recommended you."

Recommended?

Really?

She came closer to me with her laptop and showed me her screen. "Now, there are two starter packs that you need to purchase. One is $108, and the other is $50. I would recommend the $108 one."

Huh?

You have to *pay* to get hired?

"You have to *pay* to get hired?" I asked, raising an eyebrow.

"You're not getting hired, silly!" she stated. "You're starting a *business* to hire *others*!"

I guess she had a point…

"I think I'll get the cheapest starter pack," I stated.

She looked a little concerned. I couldn't tell if she was faking it or not. "Don't you want to jumpstart your business?"

"I mean, money is tight right now, and…"

"Put it on your credit card. I know you have one."

How did she know?!

"How did you…"

"You said in your business class one time, which is another thing, if you want to succeed in your business, you do *not* need to be listening to that negativity."

Who is *she* to be telling me about this?

I thought it was *my* business!

And how did she know about what I said in my business class?

"Wait, are you telling me what to *do*?" I sassed.

"No, I'm just recommending it," she lied. "Now, do you want to jumpstart your business, or not?"

Ugh, she's persistent!

"I guess…" I stated, sounding unsure.

"Okay, the $108 pack it is!" she stated and clicked on it.

"I told you, I wanted the $50 pack!" I said, starting to get angry.

"But you *just* said you wanted to jumpstart your *business*! And that requires the larger pack!" she stated. "Ali, this is an *investment* into your *future!*"

Investment?

Into my *future?!*

HOW?!

I crossed my arms, and said, "Well, if I'm getting the $108 pack, *you're* paying for a third of it."

"Sure!" she stated and went to the next page. "Now, this is where you're registering your business with ItWorks. You just need to fill this out."

Nice way to say "put in your shipping information here"...

I did as I was told, and when the checkout page hit, I passed the laptop back to her, and she passed it back to me. "You need to pay for it in *full*, and I'll pay you back what I *owe*."

Girl, you didn't mention *that*!

That's some BS!

I put in my card information and completed my registration.

From there, she showed me how to navigate the website, and how to order things....

That's it...

She took her laptop, put it back in her bag, and stated, "If you have *any* business-related questions, feel free to reach out to me or Hayden for help running your business!"

Yeah, I had a *BAD* gut feeling about *all* this...

CHAPTER 10

I found a quiet spot on campus, nestled under the shade of an old oak tree.

I needed some fresh air after spending $99 on something that will help me make more money…

Pulling out my phone, I opened Bumble, hoping for a distraction from the chaotic whirl of college and MLMs.

That's when Alex's profile popped up.

He had a laid-back vibe, his photos casual and his smile genuine. I swiped right, not really expecting much.

Almost immediately, we matched, and his first message popped up: "Hey Ali! Saw your profile and couldn't help but swipe. How's your day looking?"

I smiled, typing back. "Hey Alex, day's been a blur. Just trying to survive college and everything else."

He replied swiftly, "Tell me about it. College can be a wild ride. What are you studying?"

"Marketing major, but it's more like a major headache right now," I responded, grateful for the light conversation.

Alex sent a laughing emoji. "I get that. I'm in Computer Science. It's interesting but can get pretty dry. So, find any hidden treasures in the world of this app? I'm new on this app"

I chuckled at his question. "Mostly dick pics and blocks. You're a rare find, an actual normal person."

"So, Ali, you up for a change of scenery from this chat? Coffee sometime?" Alex's message was casual, but it held an undercurrent of genuine interest.

I hesitated, my fingers hovering over the keyboard.

Part of me yearned for this simple human connection, something normal amidst the chaos we call life.

But I just started my business…

"I'm not sure, Alex. My life's a bit of a puzzle right now. Can I get back to you on that?" I finally replied.

"Absolutely, no rush. Just thought it'd be cool to hang out. Let me know whenever," he responded, his tone still light and understanding.

I locked my phone, leaning back against the tree. The conversation with Alex was like a breath of fresh air.

As I watched students passing by, lost in their own worlds, I couldn't help but wonder about mine. Was I ready to add another piece to my already complicated puzzle?

CHAPTER 11

When I got home after school, I walked up to my room and turned on my iMac. It was around one o'clock, and I had to go on queue in about an hour.

God, I was tired…

I sat my backpack down next to me and sat down at my workstation while waiting for my iMac to boot up.

I pulled out my phone and opened up Tinder.

When I went to my messages, I noticed Hayden was typing something.

How did I know to get on at this exact moment?!

I clicked on the text thread and noticed he sent the message

Wanna come over and have some fun? ;)

Wait…

Is he asking to *hook up* with me?

That's kind of messed up…

But hey, that's coming from the girl who was imagining the same guy inside her…

"I would, but I have to work until 8. How about after?"

I INSTANTLY got a reply.

"Sorry! Wrong person lol"

I then got ANOTHER reply…

I mean, if you REALLY want to lol ;)

Ladies and gentlemen, we got him!

I get off at 8,
so I can come
over to your
place if you
want!

Same time my
parents are
leaving for a
business meeting!
You know

the address, come prepared for some good dick ;)

If he talks like that, his manhood must be THAT good!

* * *

I HATE people...

I mean, why do they have to be such ASS HOLES over the phone?

Like, who taught you to be rude to people in call centers, I can guarantee your parents didn't!

I clocked off, got on some comfy clothes, and started to walk out.

"Where are you going out this late?" Mom asked. "Don't tell me: you were now invited to an "Amway Business briefing"

"Nah, hanging out with a friend," I stated. "What's wrong with Amway?"

"Your grandmother was in it, and they are the definition of a cult," she stated. "Same with Market America, but we won't get into the CEO yelling at a tombstone at a conference telling him 'get up! I have an opportunity for you!'"

"As long as ItWorks isn't like that, I'm good."

She leaned up in her chair. "Are you entailing you *joined* ItWorks?"

Great…

Me and my loud mouth…

"*Bye!*" I started and walked out.

I'll deal with her after my guts are rearranged from some of that *good dick*.

CHAPTER 12

When I pulled up to Hayden's house, I noticed there was a car in his driveway.

Are his parents still here?

When I took another look at the car, I recognized it.

It was McKayla's car…

What was *she* doing here?

PLEASE don't tell me we're having a threesome…

I got out of my car, went up to their doorway, and knocked on the door.

McKayla IMMEDIATELY opened it up, like she was walking out.

"Oh, hey Ali! Are you here for your business review?" She asked.

Business review?

I thought I was my *own boss!*

"Yeah," I stated as she walked out and closed the door.

She threw me a smile and said "have fun!" and walked to her car.

That smile looked like Hayden gave it to her *good.*…

It made me a little worried.

As I looked away from her, I saw Hayden standing in the doorway.

"So, what's up?" he asked.

"Nothing much," I said and walked up to him. He backed up a bit and welcomed me back in.

"So, you wanna take it on the couch, or on my bed?" He asked as he closed the door.

Well shit…

That escalated quickly!

I walked up to him and kissed him on the lips. "How about you fuck me senseless on your bed."

He smiled, grabbed me by my butt, and lifted me up. "Oh, I'll give you the night of your life, baby."

He carried me upstairs to his room. His room was small and had a lot of ItWorks wrappers everywhere.

Mainly the coffee and the wraps.

He flopped me on his bed and crawled on top of me. He slowly lowered his chest onto mine, clamped my arms down on the bed, and started to kiss my neck.

Holy shit, that turned me on!

I started to moan and arched my back up as he started to nibble on my neck.

"Like that?" he asked.

"Yes," I huffed.

Hayden acted like he knew what he was doing.

His mouth trailed down my neck to the top of my breasts. His hands relinquished my wrists but only momentarily as he started to strip himself of his clothing. Pulling off his t-shirt, revealing that hardened body of his.

Then fiddling with his belt buckle, tugging that away and slipping his pants off. I followed suit, blushing brightly and just as urgent in my efforts as he is.

Eventually, both of us are in our underwear.

His bulging manhood pressed into my naked thighs as he flattened me to the bed again. Pushing the weight of his muscular physique into me and making me feel giddy with lust.

I can barely think as his mouth devoured me sweetly — going from my neck to my chest, down my body, and over my navel. Until his face is between my legs, nipping and pulling at the crotch of my panties with his teeth. My core tenses growing impatiently as I feel his hot mouth over my sex.

His breath making me tremble.

It's almost too much to bear, and I find myself hastily stripping away my bra.

Hayden peers up at me from between my legs, pressing his teeth hungrily into my mound as his eyes drank in my bare breasts. My blush deepened. The way he looked at me is so intoxicating' I can almost see all the dirty thoughts running through his imagination.

The expression on my face compelled him on. Hayden rose and dropped his boxers.

Sighing, I felt him drop the weight of his girth against the slit of my womanhood. My body thrums harder' I cannot wait any longer.

Reaching down, I pull my panties away, letting them slip and fall down my knees as my legs are bent and hanging over the side of the bed.

Hayden looks almost too smug as he looms over me with a look of lusty victory.

Before I knew it, I felt him pick my legs up and perch them on his broad shoulders before rearing back and sliding into me all in one go. The feeling of him inside me is mesmerizing.

I moan as I felt his head nestle near the back of my channel and pause for a moment allowing me to adjust to the size of him before beginning to move again. Hayden is strong and firm in his technique. Gliding into me with long, hard strokes that left me dazed. The rest of the night becomes a blur of hazy, hot sex.

CHAPTER 13

I woke up the next morning around 8:00 and turned on my computer. Today was Saturday, and I had to work from 9 am to 4 pm.

As my computer was loading, I walked downstairs to grab myself a cup of coffee.

It's the only thing that keeps me running this early in the morning....

As I brewing a cup from the Keurig, I heard some footsteps.

I looked behind and saw Mom. She was wrapped in her usual morning robe, and she looked like she had a *good* night sleep...

"Good morning," she said and grabbed a cup.

"Morning," I stated.

"I was thinking about you joining ItWorks last night while you were gone," she stated.

Yeah, gone getting some *good* dick.

"I wanted you to know that I still love you, and I want to support you throughout your life, but this is something I won't support," she stated. "Too many people fail selling for a Multi-Level Marketing company."

"I smiled, grabbed some creamer from the fridge, and said, "I'm only doing this for a little extra money. I don't expect to do this full time, like what my upline does."

"The only people that do that full time is the top 0.04% of the company," she stated and took her morning medication. "Everyone else under her is being screwed over in the butt."

Like me, last night…

"I gotcha," I stated and walked to my room.

I took a sip of my coffee, logged into my computer, and scrolled on Tik Tok, and I came across a Tik Tok from McKayla.

She was doing a Tik Tok Dance, trying to promote her business.

At the end, she posted "I only have two spots left, so hurry up and fill out the app in my bio!"

Didn't she have two spots left BEFORE I joined her?

Something's not right.

I commented on the video and said, "I joined your team, but you still have two spots left. What's up with that?"

I turned off the screen of my phone and clocked onto the phone systems we use.

Before I clocked in early, I received a message from McKayla.

Hey, I deleted your comment because we don't talk negatively about our businesses lol.

Wait…
Negativity?
How is that *negative*?!

How is that negative? I'm Not getting it…

We want people to join us! Not become haters! LOL

She's making *no* sense…

I have to get to work…

* * *

When 4'oclock hit, I was *so* happy for the day to be over! I hated that we had to say the same script over and over again to *everyone*!

As I turned off my computer, I got a text from McKayla.

**** Hey, you need to hop on this team call. You're affecting your business by not coming!****

What the fuck?

A *team call?!*

Why the fuck do I need to hop on and how is my business affected?!

I just did as I was told, and when I opened the zoom link on my phone, there were many other people there, and it looks like they were listening to someone.

It was Merik…

Why is he *always* leading these meetings?

"First off, I wanted to say welcome to all of our new business owners that decided to take the leap of faith into entrepreneurship!" He stated. "As you order your product start packs, you will fall in LOVE with the products. Unless you ordered the digital one. And to that, I say, you're not helping your business if you cheap out and buy the cheapest one."

Is he FEAR MONGERING us?

Wow…

"Now, I wanted to point out something. Since it's the end of January, you should be receiving your 1099s. Here's just a little business lesson. You can see how much you gave yourself a raise this year, by looking at box 1. That box is how many raises and bonuses you gave yourself this year!"

That…makes *NO* sense…

At all…

That money is how much money you made! *Not* how many bonuses or raises you gave yourself!

As I decided to unmute myself to try and correct her, it was disabled…

Did she disable us from proving her wrong? Probably…

CHAPTER 14

I was chatting with McKayla via texting in between calls at work, and she was giving me some tips on how I can get some people on my team.

She was telling me that I had to message random people on Instagram with a script and let them know I was open for business.

The only thing was that I couldn't create the script.

After I was done with a call, I looked at my phone, and saw she sent me the script I was to use, and told me she was going to bed.

I read over the script and cringed.

**** Hey (insert name), if you could chug a small drink twice a day, loose 2 – 3 pounds of toxic sludge in your body, combat fatigue, and feel great at the SAME TIME, would you try it?**

I have 4 spots left on my team to get a HUGE discount on thee amazing products! **

First off, I do NOT have any samples to send out.

Will she be sending me samples to send out, or do I have to buy them myself?

Because if I have to buy them, she can piss right off on that one.

And second, can I even MAKE those claims?

Is it illegal for me to be doing that?

I decided to go with the flow, follow a bunch of people, and send out the script.

After I had about 25 people, I received another call.

"Thank you for calli-"

"Hello?!" The customer stated as he cut me off.

"Yes, I'm right here sir. Thank you for ca-"

"I need to speak to someone about my service! It routed me to you!"

If this jackass doesn't let me speak, I swear…

"I apologize for the inconvenience, sir. Can you please provide me with your account information so that I can look into the issue for you?"

"Seriously? You have my number! Do your job properly and look it up that way!"

Oh, we're getting rude!

AWSOME!

My turn…

"Well sir, to protect your information, I would need this. And it's against laws regulated by the FCC for me to bypass this. Whenever you have the information, I'm ready for it."

There was a pause.

"Do you have my info pulled up yet?" He asked.

"Did you hear what I said?" I asked.

"Yes, and I-"

"Okay, so you heard me. That's good. Why are you asking me that question if you heard me?"

"Excuse me! You are NOT-"

"Sir, I don't know who you think you're talking to, but it's *not* me. If you're going to continue with this behavior, I will disconnect this call."

He was silent for a second and then the call disconnected.

Thank the lord…

I looked back on my phone, and saw I had a reply to someone.

**** I'd rather drink lighter fluid ****

I guess that's a no.

Luckily I had a script for rebuttals like that!

After I copied the script, I got another reply form someone else.

**** That sounds as appealing as a shart in the middle of a silent public gathering when you're 200 miles away from home ****

What is with these people?

Don't they know that they can make money from this business opportunity!

I sent the rebuttals, and got ANOTHER reply.

**** Sorry, I don't support pyramid schemes. ****

As I was typing out my custom reply, stating that pyramid schemes, are illegal, he blocked me Damn, people must me edgy tonight…

CHAPTER 15

The next morning, I ended up sleeping in until noon because of how late I worked.

When I got up, I tried to see if I had any new messages from people.

A lot of them had blocked me, and the rest didn't respond.

Rude!

I had a missed call from McKayla, so I called her back.

"Hey Ali! How did the messaging go?"

"Not so good. A lot of people blocked me, and the rest told me to fuck off. One of them told me he didn't support pyramid schemes."

"Did you tell him pyramid schemes are illegal and educate him on it?"

"No, he-"

She sighed, anger in her sigh. "Ali, I understand this is your first time, but you need to *work harder* at this. How many people did you message?"

Um, excuse me?

Is she *serious?*

"Are you talking to me?" I asked, prepared to go off on her.

"How many people did you message?" she repeated,

Oh, she's going there!

"I assume you're talking to me, but you're-"

"Answer the question. How many people did you message?"

Did she wake up on the wrong side of the bed?

"I'll tell you when you calm down that attitude you have."

"You're right. Now, How many people did you message?"

"About 35. 33 to be exact."

"And this is why you don't have any sales or recruits yet. You're not working hard enough."

"Exactly what do you —"

"We can talk about this later. I have money to make." She stated and hung up.

I loomed at my phone, sat it back down on my nightstand, and pinched my arm.

Was I in a fever dream, or something?

CHAPTER 16

The evening was settling in as I finally clocked out of my shift. The exhaustion of the day weighed heavily on me, but my routine of checking my phone persisted. A message from Hayden flashed on the screen.

"Hey Ali, can we talk? Something I want to ask you."

Intrigued, I found a quiet corner outside the store, the cool air a welcome change from the stifling atmosphere inside. "Sure, I'm here," I replied.

Moments later, Hayden called. His voice, usually brimming with confidence and ItWorks pitches, held a note of hesitancy tonight.

"Ali, there's this ItWorks convention coming up," he began. "It's a big deal, a lot of networking, success stories, the usual stuff. But, I was thinking, maybe you could come with me? As my date?"

The invitation took me by surprise. An ItWorks convention wasn't exactly my idea of a romantic outing. Yet, the thought of spending time with Hayden, outside the usual MLM context, was oddly appealing.

I hesitated, unsure how to respond. The world of ItWorks was overwhelming, and I wasn't sure if I was ready to dive deeper into it, even if it meant being with Hayden.

"Like a date-date?" I asked, seeking clarity.

"Yeah, a date," Hayden confirmed. "I know it's not the usual movie or dinner thing, but it could be... fun? We've been talking a lot about business and all, but I thought this could be a chance for us to, you know, spend some time together, just us."

His words hung in the air, a mix of business and personal, blurring the lines of our relationship. I found myself torn. On one hand, the idea of being with Hayden, seeing him in his element, was enticing. On the other, the shadow of

ItWorks, with all its controversies and complexities, loomed large.

"I'll think about it, Hayden," I finally said. "It's a lot to take in. I mean, an ItWorks convention as a date is *definitely* unconventional."

Hayden chuckled on the other end, a sound that eased some of my apprehension. "I know, it's weird. But I thought it could be a chance for us to get to know each other better, in a different setting. No pressure, though. Let me know what you decide."

We hung up, and I just looked at my monitor in shock and confusion.

Is he in love with me?

CHAPTER 17

After working the entire weekend, I woke up late on Monday. After that incident on Saturday, I did NOT speak to McKayla or my team for the rest of the weekend.

Until now…

I looked at my phone and saw a text from McKayla.

**** Hey Alison! Both Hayden and I think it's time for you to learn how to show people about the business! When are you free for a meeting?****

First off, do NOT call me Alison!

Only people close to me can call me that!

Everyone else can call me Ali, because they haven't earned the Alison Privilege yet.

But are we forgetting that she said "show people about the business"?

I was not in a good mood that morning from her last blowup, so I texted her back.

**** I thought this is MY business. Why do I need to "show" people THE business? ****

I got out of my bed and went downstairs.

On my way down, I got another text from McKayla.

**** It is! You have to share this business with people so that they buy stuff! And then you make money!****

Okay, that makes sense! She's teaching me how to create Facebook ads and such to get more customers!

THAT makes sense!

I got to the bottom step and texted back.

** That makes sense! What type of SEO will
we be talking about in the meeting? I have
some experience with Ads and such. **

I walked to the kitchen and got another text.

** SEO? Is that a new term for recruiting new
people? **

Is she *serious?!*

> No... It means Search
> Engine Optimization.
> If our businesses have
> a website, we NEED
> this to attract new
> customers.

I knew that lol,
Just making sure
You knew that!
And we don't need
To worry about
That. Corporate
Takes care of our

Website and stuff.
That's the beauty of
Owning your own
iWorks! Business! :)

That got me thinking…
If we're business owners, why is there a corporate office?
I'm the one that should be the corporate office!
Let me ask her…

If we're business
owners, why do
we have a
corporate office?
Shouldn't I be the
corporate office,
since I'm the
business owner?

Every business has
a corporate
office, just like
Apple, Nike, Victoria
Secrets, and every

other pyramid
scheme business
out there! The only
difference is that
nobody can be the
CEO of those companies!
We have the ability
to flow fluidly through
the company! Sounds
like you've been
listening to some haters!
I'd recommend you
do some personal
development for that! We
can go over that later though!

What the actual fuck is she talking about?
She didn't even answer my question!

You didn't properly answer.
My question. I know all
companies have a
corporate office. I was
asking why WE have

one if we're business
owners. Please answer
the question.

I then got a call from her.

"Are you going to answer the question?" I asked.

"Phew! I thought your phone got hacked by a hater! We all know how negative they can be!" She stated and giggled.

"Again, are you going to answer the question?" I asked again.

"Sounds like you need some personal development. You *really* need to stop listening to those haters. Don't let the opinions of others ruin your business." She stated.

"McKay-"

"Will you be coming over?"

"Will you answer my question?!"

"Not until you answer mine."

I've never wanted to punch someone in the face before until now...

"Yes, now can you—"

"Great! Hayden and I will see you then!" she stated and swiftly hung up.

That definitely didn't sit well with me...

* * *

When I finished eating my breakfast and watching a new YouTube video, I received a text from Hayden.

I haven't heard from him since he fucked me...

But I'll take a text from him over McKayla...

**** Hey, are you free to discuss some business stuff later tonight? ****

I could my hormones were all over the place, because that instantly horned me up...

I wanted to feel him inside me again...

So bad...

Yeah, you want round two? ;)

What? No! We need to

**Discuss with you how
To share the business
With others.**

I had the gut feeling that he wanted some of my womanhood, though.

As I put my empty bowl in the dishwasher, I got another text from Hayden.

**BUT! If you
Want "round 2",
You can
come over
After your
Business class
Today. ;)**

**I won't be back in
time for my
second class, though.**

**We can probably
Make this work.**

I had the feeling what he wanted was going be illegal…

CHAPTER 18

When I exited my business class, I was stressed.

Darlene kept arguing with everyone else about how Scentsy was the end-all-be-all.

At one point, she stated she had around $800 (or so) in "business stock" coming to her, so she can prove how good her products are.

Whatever…

I was heading to the cafeteria for a Mountain Dew, when I got a text from Hayden.

****You ready for some fun?****

What the hell is he referring to?!

In the middle of the cafeteria? I don't think that would work.

**I'm in the single-person
handicap bathroom.
Just knock three
times and say
"Occupied?" So
I know it's you.**

Holy fucking jumping Jesus on a breadstick!

He wants to fuck me in a public bathroom?!

I was about to text him back with some excuse why I couldn't, but he texted me a photo that turned me on…

Not just any photo…

A photo of his erected dick with a little but of pre-cum coming out of the tip.

I was just about to head to the main cafe, when I swiftly turned around, and headed to the back of the building where the bathrooms where.

I did as I was told — knocked not he door three times and said "Occupied?" And he opened up the door.

"Hey sexy." He sated and looked at me up and down. He bit his lip, and I walked in.

As I was walking in, he lightly smacked my ass.

"I wanna Devore that ass." He stated and took off his jacket. He put in the ground, assiniig I would lay down on it.

I've never had my ass eaten before...

I've also never had public bathroom sex before...

I turned my head, and smirked. "Only if I can suck that cock."

He stared to undo his pants, and pulled down his boxer briefs. I could see his hard cock throbbing at the sight of me.

I sat my backpack down, and got down on my knees as he walked close to me. When his dick was directly in my sight, I started to stroke it. I looked up at him, and I saw his head was thrown back.

He better not cum fast...

I moved my tongue around the tip of his dick, absorbing the taste of his sweet, salty pre-cum.

"Damn." He stated.

I put the first part of his dick in my mouth, and stated to blow him.

I could feel his manhood throb in may mouth each stroke I laid on his cock.

I stared to glide my hand under his shirt, and up to his chest. I started to feel his muscular, hard stomach, and then stared to play with his nipples.

"MM. Don't do that yet." He sated softly. "I haven't fucked you yet, baby."

I took his dick out of my mouth, and licked his erection like a lollipop.

He flowed my hand though my hair, and I stood up.

Damn, the hard concrete on my knees *really* hurt...

I placed my hands on his cheeks, and stared to make out with him.

I could tell he was a little confused why I stopped sucking, but he was going with the flow.

He slid his hands on my sides, and slid his hands on my chest, where he put the front of my shirt to the back of my neck. He then skid his hands down the back of my yoga pants. He slid my pants off my butt, and stared to feel my ass,

He stopped kissing. My lips, and laid kisses down my neck, down to my breasts where he popped one of them out of the bra, and slid his fingers down the crack between the other.

As he stated to play with my nipple on one side, he put my other nipple in his mouth.

I lightly moaned as his tongue flicked the nipple around.

He then let go, and I could tell it was ass-eating time,

I sat down on his jacket, and he climbed on top of me. I could smell the cologne he put on this morning.

Damn, the smell made things just as good.

"Damn. Ali. I'be been wanting to eat that ass *forever*." He stated and lifted up my legs, he pulled my panties out of the way, and first started to feel my butthole.

He kissed each cheek, and stared to eat me out.

Holy fuck.

I knew how it felt for things to go *out* of my ass.

But his tongue was thrusting *IN* my ass.

The orgasmic sensation caused me to moan softly, as he continued to go to town.

As he was eating me out, I heard my phone alarm go off.

That was the sign that I had to head to my next class in 5 minutes.

He soon stopped eating my ass, and moved up to my chest, while jacking off.

I could tell he was about to release.

He stuck his fingers inside me, and stated to thrust in and out.

I could tell his current motor was "If I cum, you cum too!"

I took off my shirt, and he moaned and released all over me.

He just kneeled there, panting,

"Damn." he sated and smiled at me. "You're some hot stuff for someone listening to the haters."

His fingers were still inside me as I released in his palm and all over the floor.

I just laid there, broken and tired.

I could feel his fingers slide out of me. When I looked upon, I could see him locking his fingers.

"You taste amazing." He stated. his hand was still facing himself off as he ate. "Just in time for seconds."

As I laid there, he released once more all over my chest.

He grabbed a paper towel, and handed some to me, we clean up, got dressed, and he peeked his head out.

"Clear," he stated and rushed out.

I grabbed my backpack, and headed out myself.

CHAPTER 19

Later that night

Later that night, I was getting ready for the meeting. I was spraying on some Bath and Body Works body spray, and mom came walking up to the bathroom.

All I could think about was what append in the school bathroom this afternoon…

"To *another* business meeting?" She asked me.

"Yeah, they wanted to talk to me about how to recruit people," I replied and turned around. "How do I look?"

"Like you're pretending to be a businesswoman," she replied and walked off. "Not far from the truth, you know."

She's just a hater…

I walked out of our house and headed to Hayden's place.

***

When I arrived at his place, I got out of the car and walked up to his door. I knocked on his door and waited.

And waited…

He answered the door about 5 minutes later. His hair was combed like he just got out of bed, and his clothes were all wrinkled.

"Hey, what's up?" He asked. "Come on in!"

"Nothing much," I replied and walked into the kitchen. McKayla was sitting in a chair at the kitchen table, on her phone. Her clothes were also wrinkly, and her hair was in a messy bun.

Did I walk into something?

"Hey," I stated.

She looked up from her phone and looked at me. "Hey, what's up? Ready for our meeting?"

"Yeah. Who's all gonna be here?" I asked.

"Us, and my parents." Hayden stated from behind me. As he was walking to his seat, he pinched my butt.

For some reason, I didn't flinch…It turned me on…

As I was walking to sit down next to Hayden, his parents walked in with some folders and a laptop.

Is that laptop for me?

I could use a work laptop!

They sat down next to McKayla, Merik and opened up the laptop, and then Hayden's mother gave me the folder.

"How are things going?" She asked.

"Okay, I guess. I still hate my job at the Call Center," I stated.

She looked at Merik and then said, "Well, we need to get you recruiting, so you can retire you from your 9 to 5! By the way, call me Gina!"

Retire me from my 9 to 5?

"Wouldn't that be considered quitting one job for another?" I asked.

McKayla just looked at me, and mouthed to me "Stop being a hater!"

Stop being such a HATER?!

Why does she keep telling me I'm a *hater*?!

"Not really, but we can talk about that later." McKayla spat out.

Uhh…sure….

I had a feeling this was going to be bad…

CHAPTER 20

Merik and Gina had an emergency call in the middle of the meeting, and McKayla left. I guess she assumed the meeting was over.

It just began…

Hayden said that he could help me with the recruiting in his "home office", and he led me to his room. He had rearranged his furniture so that he had a space for his desk in the corner.

I guess that was his home office, but I was more interested in that dick.

Again.

We walked into his room, and I looked around.

"How do you like the rearrangement?" He asked.

"I like it. It looks better than last time," I stated.

For some reason, his room smelled musky. Not like the typical male-smell, but like he was having sex.

It just turned me on even more.

"Well, what do you wanna do?"

I walked over to him and kissed him. "We do *that* again."

I could feel his manhood start to stick up as he scooted closer to me. He kissed me back and whispered. "Only if you stop being so *negative* and let me devour you."

Fuck yeah.

We started to make out, and he slipped his hands in my shirt. He cupped my breasts and slightly squeezed my nipples.

His hands on my bare skin felt amazing.

He slightly pushed me on his bed, and I fell on my back. He took off his shirt, revealing his muscular chest, and swiftly climbed on top of me to press his lips on mine.

He slipped off my pants, took off my panties, and spread open my legs. His gaze made me wet, as he looked at my vagina.

"Stay here." He said and walked away. He came back with a muscle vibrator.

Is he gonna…

Oh lord, things are gonna get wet…

He put his hand on the circular piece and pointed his finger out. He turned the vibrator on the max and went in.

Holy fucking shit!

The vibrations were so intense; I didn't even last 7 seconds!

My juices flew out of me, covering his chest and hand.

"Holy *fuck!*" He said, sounding shocked.

I felt miserable…

I swiftly went into the bathroom and sat down on the ground.

I knew this was natural, but hell…

"You okay?" He asked.

"Leave me *alone!*" I stated.

"I didn't know you could do that!"

"Fuck, *I* didn't know I could do that!" I stated.

"Here's this, just in case." He said through the door as he cracked it open a bit. He slid in my panties and my pants.

This went from 0 to 100 quick…

CHAPTER 21

The city's nocturnal symphony played softly outside as Hayden and I lay entwined on his couch, a comfortable silence enveloping us. His arm was loosely draped around me, a casual intimacy we had grown accustomed to. Yet, beneath the calm exterior, I sensed an unspoken tension in Hayden.

"Ali, we need to talk," Hayden's voice was hesitant, breaking the serene moment.

I shifted to face him, noticing a flicker of unease in his eyes. "What's on your mind?"

He took a deep breath, carefully choosing his words. "It's about us... this thing we have. I'm not sure it's healthy for either of us to continue like this."

His words took me by surprise. Our casual arrangement had always seemed mutually beneficial, uncomplicated. "What do you mean? I thought we were both okay with keeping things casual."

Hayden avoided my gaze, focusing on a distant point in the room. "I know, but things change, Ali. I'm starting to feel like this isn't right. We're in this limbo, and it's not fair to you or to me."

I felt a pang of confusion. Hayden had always been the one reassuring me about the simplicity of our relationship. "But Hayden, you were the one who wanted to keep things light. What's changed?"

He hesitated, then said, "I've just been doing a lot of thinking. About what I want, what's important to me. And I realize that maybe this isn't it."

I tried to read between his lines, looking for an underlying reason. "Is there someone else, Hayden?" I asked, half-jokingly.

He chuckled softly, a nonchalant shrug accompanying his response. "No, there's no one else. It's just me trying to figure things out. You know, I met someone at a networking event recently. Just a chat, but it got me thinking about where I'm heading."

I laughed, brushing off the comment. Hayden was always meeting new people, it was part of his charm. "So, you're having a mid-life crisis or something?"

Hayden didn't laugh with me. Instead, he looked more serious than before. "It's not just about that, Ali. It's about us, about what's real and what's not. I think we need to set some boundaries."

The room felt colder suddenly, the warmth of our connection dissipating. I sat up, trying to mask my growing concern. "Boundaries, right. I get it. We can keep things professional."

Hayden nodded, but there was a lingering sadness in his eyes. "I think that's for the best. For both of us."

As I left his apartment that night, his words and the subtle hints about another person lingered in my mind. I shrugged them off, convincing myself it was just Hayden being his usual, overthinking self.

But deep down, there was a nagging feeling that maybe I was missing something important, a piece of the puzzle that Hayden wasn't quite revealing.

CHAPTER 22

When I drove into my parking space, I was *not* okay.

The emotional ride I've been dealing with all day has been getting to me.

From Hayden's attitude, to the public bathroom sex, to the manipulative meeting, to the bedroom sex....

It hit my emotions, and made me feel depressed.

Like...REALLY depressed...

I walked out of my car, walked upstairs to the top floor of the complex, and reached the top of the stairs.

At that point, tears were forming in my eyes.

I hate my job, I hate my decisions, and I basically only have my mother.

Fuck it, she can survive without me...

I put the keys in the door, unlocked it, and walked in. I must have been sniffling because mom had the TV paused, and looked concerned.

"What's up?" She asked.

That was the straw that broke the camel's back because I started to cry. I bent down, putting my face in my hands.

"WHO HURT YOU?!" She yelled as she went over to comfort me. "Did that lady on TikTok send her followers to bully you ahain?!"

At this point, the thought of suicide was overtaking my thoughts.

Mom was cradling me as I was sobbing. "Mom…I can't take this anymore."

"Who…*did*…it?" She asked through closed teeth.

"Nobody," I stated and got out of her grip. I walked over to her room and pulled out Mom's semi-autimatic pistol.

I slid the bullets into the bottom, and pulled the back of it.

As I was sliding the front of the gun to my temple, I heard mom yell "ALISON! STOP!"

Before I could turn around, she was already behind me trying to get the gun out of my drip.

It was a tug-of-war between my mother trying to keep me alive and me trying to end it all…

She was winning.

"MOM!" I yelled. "I don't wanna *live* anymore! I wanna *Fucking die*! I wanna go *home*!"

"Let go of the gun!" She stated and stared to twist the gun to the ceiling.

As she was trying to twist out of my hands, the first bullet fired, leaving a hole in the ceiling.

That took me off guard, because she managed to grab the gun from me and threw it to the floor.

As I went to grab it, she tacked me to the ground and tied my arms with her belt.

She got up from my sobbing body and tied my legs with one of her long socks.

"We need to get you *help*." She stated, sounding frightened and out of breath.

I could hear her pull out her phone and dial 911.

CHAPTER 23

The police and an ambulance soon arrived, and they were talking with Mom in the other room. I was released from the tight grips of the belt and socks, and was being watched by a cop.

He was looking around, making sure there was nothing I could use to run and harm myself.

The only thing running through my mind was my urge to die.

The cop got up from mom's bed as he was looking at the doorframe. I focused my attention on the doorframe, and there was a paramedic with a stretcher.

"Ali, they're gonna take you over to Mercy South to see what's wrong." Mom stated from the doorframe.

It might be the best thing for me…

They helped me onto the stretcher and strapped me in.

Ugh, this felt so *humiliating*…

As they were wheeling me out, mom yelled from her room "I'll be right beside you! I love you!"

I love you too…

* * *

We arrived at the emergency room side of the hospital, and for the entire ride, I could see Mom's car right behind the ambulance.

She was right…

They opened the back doors, and the stretcher extended so they could wheel me inside.

After a little walk through the hallways, they led me to a room, where they told me they were gonna take my vitals.

I sat down in the chair, and a nurse came in to take my vitals.

"I'm Victoria and I'll be taking your vitals tonight." She stated and pulled up a heart rate machine. "How's your night going?"

"Not so good," I stated.

"Sorry to hear." She said softly as she took my blood pressure. She looked down at my t-shirt and said, "You sell for ItWorks?"

"Yeah."

She looked at the monitor, and said, "My cousin sells for them."

Please don't tell me she's related to *him*…

"Who's your cousin?" I asked.

"Her name is McKayla. You might know her, and her boyfriend, Hayden."

Hold up for one *fucking* second!

Did she say McKayla was her cousin?

Did she also use "boyfriend" and "Hayden" in the same *god damn* sentence?!

"What's her boyfriend's last name?" I asked, softly.

"Morris, I think. Did you know him?"

Do I *know* him?

"Yeah," I stated and shrugged. "I'm well aquatinted with not only him, but how he feels inside me."

She looked at me, confused at first.

She stared to say something, but she stopped and her eyes opened WIDE.

"Are you telling me that—"

"Yeah." I softly stated. "We had sex twice today."

She looked at my vitals and put the machine back. "Holy crap. Her boyfriend must be a *jerk* if he's cheating on such a sweet girl."

Bitch, are you *trying* to make me break down in tears?

She's NOT a sweet girl…She's a manipulative bitch.

Plus, her boyfriends dick is small…

Victoria left, and another nurse came in. "Hey Ali, follow me and we're gonna get you changed."

Changed?

Are they *admitting* me?!

I followed her to a changing area, and she handed me a cloth gown and some uncomfortable-looking, yellow socks.

"I have to watch you change." She stated.

Huh?!

I decided not to fight with her and changed into the gown and socks.

When I was done changing, she led me to an area where two other men sat, watching TV. It was like a large hallway with rooms.

"The doctor will be with you shortly. Your room is over there." She stated, pointed to my room, and left.

I just stood there and took in the cold scent. The two guys were talking, and all I could hear was the sound of the TV.

I sat down in the extra chair and watched TV.

CHAPTER 24

About an hour later, the doctor soon came in, and he took me to my room. I explained to him all that happened, and he asked questions in response as he put in the information into the laptop.

When he left to go talk to the psychiatrist, I exited the room and one of the guys was gone, while the other guy was eating a bag of chips.

I sat down next to him, and he looked at me.

"I heard bits and pieces about what happened." He stated with a mouth full of chips. He swallowed and stated. "Trust me, I know how that feels. I was in Amway for about a year, and it sounds SO familiar."

"I mean, I know Amway is basically a cult. ItWorks isn't *that* bad." I stated.

He swallowed another mouthful of chips, crumbled up the wrapper, and put it on the floor next to him. "Something that I've learned throughout my life is that those companies are scams. People recruit other people, and then make money off of their losses. That's why you were recruited. To build someone else's business."

"Well, ItWorks like I said, is different. We hire people into our businesses to promote amazing products. We don't earn *anything* off *anyone*." I stated.

For some reason, I could not feel *anything* while I was talking.

Like someone was talking through me…

He looked in the other direction, and then back at me. "I know you're just taught to say this stuff, but that's *not* how it is. According to our own federal government, 99.6% of people lose money with these types of companies," He stated. "And if it's anything that makes me mad, it's ignorance."

"No, I agree. Ignorance makes me mad too. That's why I am trying to build my team to teach those ignorant haters that 99.6% of people don't work hard enough in their businesses."

"Do you *hear* yourself?!" He stated and laughed a little.

"Yeah. Do you know what opportunity you're missing out on?" I asked like I was trying to recruit him.

He slammed the back of the plastic chair and stormed off. "Nobody wants to join your *fucking pyramid scheme!!!*"

It was then that reality hit me, and I thought to myself.

Maybe he's right…

CHAPTER 25

The next day

They let me go that night, and I arrived at school the next day. I headed into the business building, and I was still a little ashamed about what happened last night.

On my way to my business development class, I passed a career fair!

Could this be my time to get out of my call center?

Maybe!

I looked around through the booths, took some business cards, and then went on my way.

As I was walking to my class, I saw Hayden.

God, I didn't want to think about what happened....

"Hey," I stated.

"Were you at the career fair getting business cards?" He asked.

"Yeah, why?"

"I didn't even think of that! We could call up or email those people on your business cards and pitch them the business!"

Uh, I think the fuck NOT!

"Actually, I was trying to get out of the call center role that I'm in," I stated.

He looked a little angry at that point. "I thought you were going to work your business to do that?"

"Yeah, but…"

"What you *need* to do is to recruit more people into your business to become financially free. Then you won't need to be searching for another job." He stated and walked off.

What the fuck is *his* problem?

I caught up to him and said, "I'm just trying to better myself."

"I think you need to do some more personal development. It seems like you don't trust the business enough." He stated.

That stopped me in my tracks.

Why is he acting this way?

I stopped walking, and he walked off.

* * *

I arrived at my classroom and sat down at my desk. I still couldn't believe how rude he was to me!

One by one, the students walked in, and the thought of our conversation kept bothering me more and more.

What was his problem?

Why did he act like that?

Did I do something last night that offended him?

Does he not like me anymore because of me trying to get another job?

As I was pondering to myself, Professor Casva walked in, sat his backpack down, and wrote on the board "WARM-UP QUESTION: WHAT IS THE DIFFERENCE BETWEEN A LEGAL AND ILLEGAL PYRAMID SCHEME?"

I could tell that the question pissed Darlene off.

"Professor, what's a legal pyramid scheme?" She asked.

"A Multi-Level Marketing company," He stated back. "I'll be right back." He stated and walked out.

She huffed, and said under her breath, "MLM's can't be legal pyramid schemes, because we can surpass our recruiter."

"That literally has *nothing* to do with the business structure, shit head" Isabella stated as she was writing on her paper.

Darlene turned around and stated, "Girl, you WORK for a pyramid scheme, so I'd advise you be *shut the fuck up* about this."

Isabella looked up. "I *literally* work for TJ Max…"

"Yeah! You have the CEO at the top, the executives under him, the district managers under them, the managers under them, and then you. At the bottom of the pyramid." She stated. "So yes, your 9-to-5 *is* a *pyramid* scheme."

"Girl, how *fucking* stupid *are* you?" Isabella asked and put her hair in a ponytail.

Please don't tell me they're gonna throw hands…

"That's literally the *corporate hierarchy*! What everyone has a problem with is the *business structure!*" She stated.

"Sorry, but you're misinformed. You're just being a *hater,*" Darlene stated and turned around.

"If hating on an industry that is set up for people to fail is bad, then fuck me in the ass without lube." The quiet kid stated.

Darlene looked at him. "Don't think you're off the hook from spreading *so much* misinformation from *last* time we had a discussion about this."

"I'm sorry, but *misinformation*? I literally got my information from the Federal trade commission. Where did you get *your* information?" He asked.

She huffed again. "You people need to stop being such haters! Except Ali; she knows what it's like to be a business owner."

"Excuse me, but *why* are you bringing *me* into this?!" I asked, sounding panicked. "I don't sell your wax melts!"

"We know you don't. You sell for itWorks under your new friend McKayla."

I have *never* had the urge to beat someone's ass before until now.

Isabella looked at me in fear. "Ali? Why would you join a pyramid scheme?!"

I was panicking now.

I swiftly packed up my things to get the fuck out of here before I panic, again.

"Where you going?" Darleen asked.

"Don't know, but we know you're *fucking* going to *hell* for making her uncomputable like that." Isabella sated and closed her laptop.

I put the backpack over my shoulder, and rushed out.

CHAPTER 26

I was speed-walking down the hall with a flood of emotions and thoughts going through my head.

What the actual, living fuck was that for?!

How did she know I singed up for ItWorks?!

Why did the think I wanted everyone to know?!

After Hayden and I had sex in the fucking bathroom, I didn't want *anyone* knowing that I sold ItWorks! At this college…

ESPECIALLY that class!

While I was walking down the hall, I heard a voice.

"Ali! Wait!"

I turned around with my tear-filled eyes, and turned my head behind me.

Isabella was chasing me.

I stopped in my tracks and turned around.

"Before you get too upset, I wanted to say I was sorry."

"Why would she *say* that and expose the side of me I'm *ashamed* of?" I asked and started to break down.

I had *no* idea that I felt this way…

How could an industry break someone this much?

I sat down next to the wall and started to cry silently. Isabella sat next to me and put her arm around me.

"And the worst part is, I think I'm in love with my upline's upline!" I stated under tears.

I could hear a huff come from Isabella. "That's how they get you in."

Huh?

I looked at her. "What do you mean?"

"Have they treated you like the British Royal Family since joining?"

"I mean, if having your upline stick his dick inside of you is considered being treated like royalty, then yes."

Her eyes flew open. "You mean to tell me that your upline's form of love-bombing is to *fuck* you?!"

"Not my *direct* upline. Her upline," I stated.

I then proceeded to spill the entire cannot beans to her. From the disabled mics in the Zoom session, to constantly labeling me as a hater, to the sex.

"First, you're *not* a *hater*. That is what they label anyone that "talks bad" about the business. Second, them disabling the unmute button is a form of manipulation and information control.

In a model to identify cults by Steven Hassen called "The BITE model", that can be part of "Information Control" because they are not only preventing you from learning the truth, they are lying to you.

And the sex…That's just…I mean… *so fucked up*! What's his name?"

"Hayden Morris."

She threw her head back and lightly hit the wall. She huffed and then mumbled under her breath "*Not the Morris'…*"

"What's wrong with them?" I asked.

"*Many* things are *fucked up* with that god-awful family. First, they're *toxic* as *fuck*. They will do *anything* to manipulate and gaslight the shit out of you to join their pyramid scheme. Gina is in an active lawsuit with another legitimate business for harassing their employees to join their *fucking* cult. Rumor has it that Merik is cheating on his wife with some crack whore. They're also money-hungry, and are overall *terrible* for society."

"What about Hayden? Their son." I asked. I was starting to tone down on the crying.

She pied her face with her hands. "Please tell me he isn't the one who fucked you."

"Yeah, why?"

She paused. She looked angry. "He's the *pure* definition of a raging whore. He originally lived out on his own, but *another* rumor has it that he got kicked out because he kept trying to recruit people into his *former* MLM and then love-bombed them by offering sex to them."

Holy fuck!

"Hold on, *what*?!" I asked.

"That's not *all*! He also illegally buys his ranks at ItWorks!, so he seems more successful than he *actually* is. He was able to bring a girl named McKlayla over from the other MLM with him."

"McKayla Payton?" I asked.

She looked concerned. "Shit, I'm scared to ask. How do you know her?"

"She's my direct upline."

Isabella bumped the back of her head to the wall again and huffed loudly. "Jesus *fuck*! We need to get you out of their cult. And we need to get you out, like, now!"

"How?" I asked.

Isabella got up and helped me up. "After class, meet me in the library and we can discuss a game plan to get you out. First, we need to get back to class before Professor Casva gets back in."

CHAPTER 27

After class, Isabella and I were sitting in a study room at the library, and she was giving me a LOT of useful information about MLM's. From studies to real-life examples of manipulation tactics, to YouTube videos of different creators "Spilling to tea"

"Now, it looks like in order to quit being an ItWorks distributor, you have to dial this number and require to quit. I believe they will also cancel any subscriptions you may have." She stated. "Have you bought any products through them yet?"

"Not yet."

"You lucky soul." She replied. "Most people get invested and buy thousands of dollars in products." She stated. "I have to get going in about twenty minutes, so we have time if you want me to stay here."

"Sure," I said and dialed the number.

I chose the appropriate phone options and got connected to a representative.

"Thank you for calling the independent business owner support line at ItWorks, my name is Mia, how can I help you?" Mia said on the other end.

"Yes, I need to cancel my distributorship with ItWorks," I stated.

"Certainly. Just wanted to let you know that if you have any active auto-shipments that you would like to cancel early, you will be required to pay a $50 one-time fee to cancel." She stated. "I see you have three auto-shipments on your file. One was for the Hair, Skin, and Nails that was placed…Looks like…Two hours ago by the authorizing representative McKayla, another is an order for the Keto Coffee and the Sleepy Tea, by the authorizing representative Hayden."

Whoa, whoa, WHOA!

WHAT?!

"I did not authorize those," I stated.

"No worries, since they were placed within 24 hours, I can cancel them without you having to pay the fee. One second." She stated and placed me on hold.

"I rolled my eyes and placed the phone on speakerphone.

"What happened?" Isabella asked.

"McKayla and Hayden placed orders on my account," I stated.

"They fucking WHAT??!" She asked.

"Yeah."

"You can sue for that! That's fucking red —"

"Thank you for holding, I have successfully canceled your auto-shipments, and I have processed your cancelation for your business. You and your upline should be receiving an email about this confirmation. Is there anything else I can help you with today?" She asked.

"I think that's it," I stated.

"Thank you for calling and have a good day," Mia stated and hung up.

I could feel a pressure lift off my chest; like a thousand-pound weight was lifted off me.

Like I was free from jail!

"Well, you did it," Isabella stated. "Now the only thing to do is to block McKayla and Hayden."

"Actually, not yet," I stated.

She looked confused. "What for? They're going to harass you to the end of your life."

"Not until I get my revenge," I stated.

CHAPTER 28

The afternoon sun cast a warm glow over the quaint streets as I made my way to my mom's workplace. My mind was a tumultuous sea, thoughts of ItWorks and Hayden crashing against each other.

The need to talk to someone, to seek advice, felt urgent, and my mom, with her no-nonsense wisdom, was the first person who came to mind.

The bell above the door jingled as I entered the small bakery where my mom worked. She was behind the counter, her hands skillfully decorating a cake. Spotting me, she gave a warm, knowing smile.

"Ali, what a surprise! Everything okay?" she asked, her eyes reflecting concern.

I took a seat at one of the tables, the familiar scent of freshly baked bread enveloping me. "Mom, I need to talk. It's about ItWorks... and Hayden."

She finished up with the cake and came over, pulling up a chair. "Who's Hayden? And what about them?" she said, her voice steady.

I poured out everything – the doubts, the realizations, the pressures of being part of ItWorks, and my complicated relationship with Hayden. Speaking it all aloud made the burden feel heavier, yet necessary.

My mom listened intently, her expression a mix of empathy and worry. When I finished, she reached across the table, taking my hand in hers.

"Ali, it sounds like you've been carrying a lot on your shoulders. This ItWorks shit, this Hayden guy... they're not worth your peace of mind."

I nodded, feeling the truth in her words. "I know, Mom. It's just hard. I invested so much time and energy into this, and Hayden... I thought there was something real there."

She squeezed my hand gently. "Sometimes, we get so caught up in what we think we should do, we lose sight of what's best for us. It's okay to walk away, to start fresh."

Her words resonated with me, offering clarity amidst the chaos. "You think I should end my contract with ItWorks? Cut Hayden out?"

"Only you can make that decision, Ali. But remember, it's your life, your future. You need to do what's best for you, not for anyone else."

We sat in silence for a while, the bakery's cozy atmosphere a comforting embrace.

"Let's go home, sweetie. We'll figure this out, together. It's time for me to go anyway" mom said as she took off her apron.

CHAPTER 29

When I got home, I put my backpack on the couch and opened up my laptop. I opened up my email and noticed I had two exciting emails sitting for me.

One was the email confirming that I quit ItWorks.

And the other was from T-Mobile!

Dear Ali,

Thank you for applying to work at our cooperate office in our marketing team! We would like to extend an invitation to have a virtual interview with our team and see if you're a good fit for the Un-Carrier!

CLICK HERE to schedule your interview.

Thank you,
T-Mobile Recruiting.

YES!

I can get out of my call center job!

I clicked on the link, and scheduled my interview.

I couldn't believe it!

I was *finally* getting a chance to get out of the call center industry!

The thought of that made me tear up a bit.

As I was wiping my tears off my eyes with my shirt, Mom walked in.

"Ali! Are you okay?!" He asked and stared to rush to me.

I looked up at her, and stated. "T-Mobile is offering me a job in marketing!"

She smiled, and rushed over to me, she sat next to me, and looked at the computer monitor.

"Holy shit!" She screeched and hugged me. "I knew you could do it! I had faith in you!"

I stared to cry in her shoulder.

I wasn't sad.

I was happy.

"Thank you." I stated under teary eyes. "I have some other news as well."

"Are they going to pay for your schooling?"

"Nope. I sent in my resignation email to itWorks! With a new friend this afternoon."

She smiled at me and hugged me again. "I'm so glad you got out!"

For some reason, I was *shocked* ay her reaction.

I was told that people against MLMs wouldn't act like this when we told them they quit.

"I didn't know how you would act when I said that." I stated. "I thought you would be negative about it, like all those other MLM haters."

"Ali, people who don't agree with the business model of MLM's are just people with a different viewpoint. Personally, I'm always happy and exited for someone when they get out." She stated and got up. "Wanna go to Olive Garden to celebrate?"

"Sure!"

CHAPTER 30

We were sitting at Olive Garden waiting for our food. Mom was snacking not he breadsticks, and I was on my phone.

I was scrolling through my For You Page, when I got a message form someone in the app.

**** Hey Ali! Listen, we don't know each other, but I noticed you're very ambitious, and you're looking for something you can do on your terms and around your schedule. I'm looking to expand one of my online stores and looking to work with 10 people who want to earn 50% commissions UP FRONT! Would you like to know more? If not, let me know! No hard feelings! ****

Mom must have noticed me reading, and she asked, "Who you talking to?"

"Nobody. This random guy sent me a message on TikTok. He's talking about something I can do from home and earn 50% commission up front."

"Sounds like another pyramid scheme, but I've *never* heard of an MLM company that pays THTA much. I know Sceitn paid sixty percent, but not fifty percent. Message him and ask him it's an MLM."

I did as I was told, and accepted his request.

**** Is it some sort of MLM? I'd prefer not to scam innocent people. ****

As he was typing, I was googling him.

It didn't seem like he was apart of an MLM that I could *tell…*

He was a Brand Ambassador for some company called Melaleuca, but I have *never* heard of them.

"He's a brand ambassador for some company called Melaleuca." I stated.

"Interesting let me see what I can find." She stated and got out her phone.

I was about to google as well, when he sent me a message.

**** No, We're not an MLM. We are a referral club. You refer people to shop at your link, and you get a kickback. ****

He also sent a zoom link and told me to join in 3 minutes, as they were staring soon.

"He says no to the MLM, but they're a Referral club of some sort. He sent me a zoom link." I stated.

"Join it and let me know. I see mixed results about this company."

Our food then came, and we ate as I was listening to the zoom.

* * *

When we were finished eating, they just got done explaining the comp plan.

Throughout the *entire* time I was eating, I was getting *massive* MLM vibes.

I took out my airpiods, and said, "It sounds like one."

Mom paid for our food with the little kiosk machine, and looked at me while the receipt was printing. "Is this the first MLM cold message you have ever received?"

"No. McKayla messaged me to join itWorks before Hayden did."

"Hayden? Who's he?"

I then explained the entire story, but minus the sex.

"I'm jet glad you're out." She stated and singed the receipt.

As we were walking out, I got another DM form this guy.

**** Hey, I saw you left the zoom call while he was talking. What happened?****

Oh yeah…
I didn't tell him.

> **I left because it sounded like a pyramid scheme. And I told you I don't do those.**

So what I hear is that you don't
like corporate America?
You don't like supping
small businesses?
I can always weed
out the negative
ones from the
positive, open-minded
 people.

I'm sorry…WHAT?!
The lion, the witch, and the motherfucking
audacity of this bitch!

> No, I support small businesses.
> That's why I don't mess
> with MLM's/Pyramid
> schemes like Melaleuca.
> And you're talking about
> the corporate hierarchy
> and comparing it to the
> business structure. Do
> a quick google search

before saying something
so goddamn stupid.

LOL I'm going to the same
college as you for business,
entrepreneurship,
and marketing. ALL of
my professors, especially
Professor Casva, say
this is a small
business and NOT
an MLM! *SOMEONE*
wasn't paying attention

Well, considering our
Community college lets
Us only take ONE degree
Program at a time, I
Highly doubt you're going
To the same one as me
Wile taking three degree
Programs. I doubt you're

Going to a community
College AT ALL! And
I have professor Casva,
And he has NEVER ONCE
Said that an MLM is a small
business. He says the opposite.
Also, explain why you have
to recruit (or as you say, refer)
people to share their link in
order to get paid? Sounds like
an MLM, but okay…

Sorry but not sorry,
But I only hire educated
And business-save
Entrepreneurs into
MY business. Sounds
Like to me you're not
Cut out for this amazing
Business!

Okay, and I only let guys

Inside me with
fat dicks. Sounds
Like to me you're not
Cut out for this
Amazing pussy.

I admit, that was harsh…

But hey, anything to get him to shut the fuck up…

CHAPTER 31

I was seated at the kitchen table, surrounded by a mess of papers and my laptop, deep in preparation for my upcoming job interviews.

My mom was there, offering her usual blend of stern guidance and supportive encouragement.

Every now and then, she'd chime in with a helpful suggestion or a much-needed critique.

In the midst of discussing potential interview questions, my phone buzzed with a notification.

It was a message from Alex on Bumble. Seeing his name brought an unexpected smile to my face, a brief respite from the stress of job hunting.

"Hey Ali! Long time no chat. How have you been? Fancy catching up over coffee next week?"

I hesitated for a moment, glancing at my mom who was busy sifting through a pile of notes.

"Go on, reply," my mom said, noticing my distraction. "It's okay to take a break and have some fun."

Encouraged by her words, I typed back a response.

"Hey Alex, it's been a while! Coffee sounds great. How's next Saturday for you?"

The conversation with Alex flowed easily, a stark contrast to the tension and uncertainty that had colored my recent interactions with Hayden.

We settled on a cozy café downtown for next Saturday, and the plan for a casual coffee date was set.

As we continued chatting, I felt a lightness in my spirit. Alex's easygoing nature and genuine interest were refreshing. It felt good to engage in something normal, something simple.

After finalizing our plans, I turned my attention back to the interview prep. My mom gave me a knowing look, a mix of approval and motherly concern.

"Alex seems like a nice guy," she commented.

I nodded, feeling a sense of hope and anticipation for the first time in a long while. "Yeah, he does. It'll be nice to get to know him better."

CHAPTER 32

It was the day of my interview, and I was in the parking lot of the building. My interview was in 10 minutes, and I was just waiting.

As I was watching someone talk about their MLM story in some southwestern MLM, I got a text,

It was McKayla.

**Hey, did you cancel your
business on accident?
We got an email stating
you quit…**

**Yeah, I quit ItWorks. I
Couldn't take Hayden
Constantly wanting
To have sex with me
Anymore. His dick is
Small, and he's very
Unprofessional for
Wanting to have sex**

With me multiple times.
But you would know.
He's your boyfriend.

With that, I blocked both of them, got out of the car, and walked into the building.

It was time for me to move on to bigger and better things in my life…and playing business owner isn't coming along.

www.ingramcontent.com/pod-product-compliance
Lightning Source LLC
Chambersburg PA
CBHW031140130726
47988CB00006B/2458